CH

To the friends who have helped me through dark times.

Boy Seeking Band is published by Stone Arch Books
1710 Roe Crest Drive, North Mankato, Minnesota 56003
www.mycapstone.com

Cataloging-in-Publication Data is available on the Library of Congress website.
ISBN: 978-1-4965-4446-9 (library hardcover)
ISBN: 978-1-4965-4450-6 (eBook)

Summary: After transferring from a private arts school to a public school,
prodigy bass player Terence Kato is finishing eighth grade on a low note, until
he starts building a rock band! With a singer signed on, he's ready to scale up
the band even more by finding a KEYBOARDIST.

Cover illustration and design by Brann Garvey

Printed in the United States of America.
010368F17

KEYBOARDIST WANTED

BY STEVE BREZENOFF

STONE ARCH BOOKS
a capstone imprint

TABLE OF CONTENTS

INTRODUCTION

Terence Kato is a prodigy bass player, but he's determined to finish middle school on a high note. Life has other plans. In the middle of eighth grade, he's forced to transfer from a private arts school to a public school, where the kids seemingly speak a different language. Luckily, he knows a universal one: music. He quickly sets out to build the city's greatest band.

With a singer already signed on, Terence is ready to scale up the band even more by finding a KEYBOARDIST.

CHAPTER ONE

It's Monday morning, and Terence
Kato — former high-class art-school hot-shot
and currently enrolled at public Franklin Middle
School — has had a band with fellow eighth-
grader Meredith "Eddie" Carson for exactly
sixty-seven and a half hours.

Terence hunches his shoulder against the
January chill and shoves his hands deeper into
the pockets of his hoodie. He wishes he had his
gloves, or rather, he wishes he knew where his

gloves were. But with the move from the old house to the rental, eighty percent of his stuff — and his dad's stuff — remains in boxes in the corner of their living room.

Neither he nor his dad relished the idea of opening any of those boxes, whatever the need, because what if they opened a box full of Mom's stuff? Terence doesn't think he can handle that. He *knows* Dad can't handle it.

Terence hears the bus before he sees it. Next comes a poof of thick gray smoke just before the front of the bus peeks over the hill on the next block. It seems to take forever to chug its way along. The brakes squeak and the doors open with an airy *thwack*, and Terence climbs aboard.

Eddie saved him a seat.

"Good morning, bandmate!" she says, sliding over for him and grinning madly. Eddie grins madly a lot, Terence has learned in his first week at Franklin Middle. In fact, she seems to do everything a little madly, including dress herself. Today she's wearing a black, white, and gray patched skirt over red jeans and a black Beatles T-shirt over a green thermal.

In her hands, she's got a black three-ring binder, decorated with puffy stickers and drawings and scribblings in Wite-Out. The biggest one — right in the middle, in thick cursive — says "Songs."

"Hi," Terence says. "Um . . . what's that you've got there?"

She pats the cover affectionately. "This is my song book," she says. "I don't know when we'll get to play again, but I thought I could show you some of these."

"Sure," Terence says slowly. "I mean, I'd like to hear them. Do you play guitar too?"

She shakes her head. "Well, a little," she says. "I'm just good enough to play some chords to back myself, you know? Just to write the melodies." She slumps in her seat in a little.

"I'm so relieved. I thought you would think it was silly."

"Songwriting, silly?" Terence says. "Of course not. Why would I think that? It's great that you write songs. Someday you can form your own band and perform them, when you're ready."

"Wait, what?" she says.

Terence straightens in his seat and looks at the back of the seat in front of them. "I just mean, you know, this is *my* band."

"Oh, is it?"

He nods. "I have a set list all planned, is the thing," Terence says. "It's the same one we played in my old band."

"At the private school."

"At Hart Arts, yeah," Terence says. "If those songs were good enough for the virtuosos at Hart, they'll be good enough for you, right?"

Eddie's smile falls away for an instant, but then she's right back to grinning, her lip-glossed

12

mouth stretched into madness. "Right," she says, slipping her binder back into her bag.

"So I was thinking," Terence says, "I can play piano for practicing a little, but I'm better on bass, and I prefer it, so we should find a keys player right away."

Eddie stares out the window as the bus rolls along Riverside Drive.

"Eddie?" Terence says.

"What?" she says. "Oh, a piano player. Right. For sure."

"Do you know anyone who plays?" Terence asks.

"Just you," she says.

Terence smirks.

"I'll ask Luke," Eddie says.

"Um, I don't know if that's a good idea," Terence says, twisting in his seat to check out her brother sitting at the back of the bus with his big, scary friends.

They're all acting crazy, swinging on the

seats, shouting and throwing pencils at each other.

Except Luke. He's just sitting in the aisle seat and staring — at Terence.

"I think he's going to eat me," Terence says, straightening in his seat again.

"Oh, stop," Eddie says. "He's just . . . confused. You're weird."

"Right, I keep forgetting."

"Anyway, he's been playing sax since second grade," Eddie says. "Even if he's not very good. He's bound to know someone who plays piano after all those years."

"If you say so," Terence says. The bus pulls up to the curb in front of Franklin Middle. "Listen, I'm quitting jazz band."

"What?" Eddie says as they shuffle down the bus aisle to climb off. "Bonk's going to cry."

"Doubt it," Terence says. "He doesn't like my improvisational style anyway."

A few teachers are holding the doors open

as the buses arrive, like every day, and Terence and Eddie mumble good-mornings and accept flaccid high fives.

"Besides," Terence continues, following Eddie to her locker, "if I have after-school stuff every day, when will we ever practice?"

"It's your life," Eddie says as she opens her locker and drops off her book bag, save a notebook and textbook, which she shoves under one arm. She slams the locker. "See you at lunch?"

"Sure," Terence says, and Eddie skips down the hall.

Terence turns to head to his advisory class — and walks right into the ample, wall-like chest of Luke.

"Watch it," Luke says.

"Sorry," Terence says, moving to go around the cinderblock wall of a boy.

Luke grabs his arm. "You better be nice to her."

"I will!" Terence says, struggling to free himself from Luke's grip. "I mean, I am!"

Luke releases him, grunts menacingly, and stomps off.

"Great," Terence mutters to himself and he plods toward advisory. "That guy's our primary source for a keys player. This ought to be good."

"You talkin' to yourself, weirdo?"

Terence looks up and finds a pair of boys as big as Luke, and twice as mean looking. They stand shoulder to shoulder, blocking his path.

"Hey, you're that new kid," says the uglier one. His nose looks like he might have played pro hockey in a previous life. "The one from Hart Arts and Farts."

"I just want to get to class," Terence says, keeping his eyes on the floor.

"Oh, you're not going to class," says the bully on the left, grinning down at Terence. He reaches out slowly, takes Terence by the front of his shirt, and lifts him off the ground.

The other bully steps around behind him and snatches his book bag.

"Come on!" Terence protests as the first boy drops him.

Together, they open his bag and dump the contents all over the floor. At the same moment, the late bell rings.

The two bullies stand over Terence as he crouches to pick up his stuff.

"We're just gonna dump it again," says one.

But just then, high heels click and clack around the corner. Principal Stone appears and puts her hands on her hips.

"Aren't you two going to help him pick up his things?" she says.

The bullies almost seem like they will, but Terence quickly shoves the books and papers and pens back into his bag and rises. "I'm fine, Ms. Stone," he says.

"Good," she says with an icy glare. "Now get to class, all of you."

The bullies hurry off. Principal Stone puts a hand on Terence's shoulder before he can scamper off. "And no more tardiness, either. You're new, but by now you ought to know what time class starts, OK?"

"Sorry," Terence says, hurrying away.

CHAPTER TWO

Unlike back at Hart Arts — a school whose focus was strictly on the arts and where the core curriculum of math, science, history, and language took a backseat — here at Franklin Middle the arts are completely ignored.

Sure, there are drawing electives and the after-school jazz band. But the classes — the hours every student put in between 7:30 and 2:30, aside from lunch — were all core curriculum. Back at Hart, Terence might have spent the whole morning in a little sealed room with three other students, a piano, a double bass, maybe a couple horns.

The negatives of this change for someone like Terence are obvious. But there are positives too. This morning, the main positive is that Terence moves from class to class, seeing nearly every student in eighth grade.

"Hi," Terence says to the boy at the next desk as he takes his seat in the back of Mr. Ellison's social studies class.

"Um," the boy says, looking around a little, "hi?"

"I'm new," Terence says.

"I know."

"I was wondering," Terence says, "do you know anyone who plays piano?"

The boy stares at him blankly for a long moment before finally saying, his face contorted in confusion, "I don't think so. Do we need a piano player in social studies class?"

"No," Terence says. "Not usually."

"Oh, good," the boy says, settling into his seat and facing the teacher at the front of the class.

Terence takes part in several equally awkward conversations throughout his day. In study hall — which students are forced to spend in one lecture hall in relative silence, compared to study hall at Hart when Terence would would have spent the time in a practice space jamming with Polly and the others — Terence leans along the aisle of the lecture hall.

"Hey," he whispers to a nearby girl.

The girl looks at him briefly. "Hi," she says, smiling. "Hey, you're the new boy. The weird one, right?"

Terence almost rolls his eyes, but she's smiling at him, and he thinks he recognizes her as a girl in his first-hour math class. "Some people think so."

The girl twists her neck to look back at Mr. Ghoti, the study-hall monitor. Then she grabs her book bag and purse from the seat between them and hops into the seat to be next to Terence.

"So what's your *story*?" she says, leaning on the armrest between them. "Where'd you come from? Aliana says you moved here from Russia, but that's obviously not true."

She leans a little closer.

"Right?"

Terence leans back and checks to make sure Mr. Ghoti is still distracted by the magazine he's reading.

"Um, right," Terence says. "I'm definitely not from Russia. Actually, I've always lived around here. We just moved from across town." He swallows and adds even more quietly, "And I had to change schools."

"Tell me everything about your old school," the girl says. "Was it as horrible as this place?"

Terence thinks about Hart Arts — his friends there, his band, the music, the relaxed atmosphere, hallways full of singing. But he doesn't say any of this.

"Actually," Terence says, straightening in his seat, "I was just wondering if you know anyone who plays piano."

She stares back at him, her mouth hanging open.

"Sorry, I just . . . ," Terence says, stammering a little, "I just don't feel like chatting right now." *Especially about Hart.*

"OK," she says, flinching as if he slapped her. Her voice now is icy and cracks like the top of a frozen puddle when you step on it. "No need to be rude."

"No, it's nothing like that," Terence says as she hops back into her original seat, stuffing her book bag between them again. "It's just that I'm not super interested in making friends here."

She glances at him as she opens the textbook in her lap and then puts her eyes on a completely random page.

"At Franklin, I mean," he says.

"Mmhm," she says, not looking up. "Not chatting."

"Right," Terence says. "But, um . . . do you? Know anyone?"

She slams her book closed and glares at him. "Melody Ulrich," she says, frigid, and then raises one finger and points to a girl at the bottom of the lecture hall. "Her."

Melody sits alone in the front row. She wears earbuds, has a notebook in her lap, a textbook open on the seat on her left and another on the right.

"Thanks," Terence says, and he gathers his stuff and makes his careful way along the aisle.

"Melody?" Terence says, sliding into the seat behind the girl.

She doesn't reply.

Terence taps her on the shoulder and she jumps and turns around. "What?" she snaps, pulling an earbud out.

"Sorry," Terence says. "Are you Melody?"

"So?" she says.

"Well," Terence says, getting nervous now as Melody seems to get more angry, "I hear you play piano."

"Are you trying to be funny?" Melody says.

Terence thinks for a second. "Am I being funny?"

Melody rolls her eyes. "Yes, I play piano. I've been playing piano since I was three years old. Everyone knows I play piano, OK?"

"OK."

"What are you, new here or something?" Melody says, pushing her earbud back in.

"Yes, actually," Terence says, kind of pleased that someone in his class at Franklin *doesn't* know he's the new, weird kid.

Of course Melody doesn't hear him, since her earbud is back in. But Terence hasn't even had a chance to mention the band yet. He taps her shoulder again.

"What?" she snaps, again tugging her earbud out.

"I'm starting a band," Terence says.

"Good for you."

"And we need a piano player," Terence adds.

Her face softens a bit. "Oh," she says. "You want *me*?"

Terence shrugs a little. He was sure he at least wanted to hear her play a few minutes ago, but now . . . "I was hoping you'd audition."

She closes the book on her lap and pulls out her other earbud. "I don't need to audition."

"You don't?"

She shakes her head. "I'm the best pianist at Franklin, probably better than the ham-fisted players at the high school too."

"Still," Terence says. "I should probably hear you play."

The bell to end study hall rings, and Melody starts packing up her books as she stands. "Suit yourself," she says. "Come to my house this afternoon. I have a fifteen-minute window at 4:30, after my Latin tutor and before my krav maga class."

"Krav ma —?" Terence starts to say. "Sure. 4:30. Can do."

"Give me your phone."

Terence obeys, and Melody quickly types in her number and address. "See you."

With that, she hurries off to her next class.

Terence gathers his stuff and leaves the lecture hall.

"Hey, Weird Terry." It's Eddie, waiting just outside the lecture hall, ready to pounce. "Tell me you didn't just ask Melody Ulrich to join our band."

"I might have," Terence says slowly. "Why?"

Eddie sighs. "Look, forget about her," she says. "Luke's friend Claude can do it."

"Luke's friend?" Terence says. "I don't know. . . ." He looks over Eddie's shoulder. Luke is there, a little way down the hall and in close conversation with another big guy who must be Claude.

Claude is a little taller than Luke, and broader too. He's wearing black jeans, big black boots, and a black denim jacket open to reveal a ragged-looking white T-shirt bearing a grinning skull. His black (of course) hair is long and greasy looking.

"Him?"

Eddie glances and waves. The boys don't wave back. "Him," Eddie says.

"Look, let's just hear Melody play," Terence says. He can probably get used to having Luke around now and then, but a boy even bigger than Luke, twice as scary, and playing keys for *his band*? No way, especially after his run-in with Tweedledum and Tweedledee before advisory this morning. Those two sure seemed like the kind of guys Luke hangs out with.

"I've heard Melody play," Eddie says with a straight face. "She's amazing."

Terence cocks his head. "OK then," he says. "Then she's the one for us, right?"

"I didn't say that."

The bell rings, sending kids all around hurrying to their next classes. "Look, I'm going to hear her play at her house today. You should come."

"I told you," Eddie says as Terence backs away, anxious about being late to class. "I've heard her."

"Come anyway?" Terence says.

He hurries away, Eddie calling after him, "Fine! But it's a waste of time!"

Not long ago, if Terence Kato needed to get to a friend's house clear across the neighborhood — especially on a windy, snowy winter night — Terence would have asked his father for a ride.

It's funny. Even then, Mom wouldn't have been around, not by four in the afternoon, anyway. She'd be working, if she was even in town.

Even so, things happened. Dad got things done. He gave Terence rides when he needed them, made dinner, cleaned up the house.

At 4:30 this afternoon though, with the snow picking up and the sun setting, Terence stops his bike in front of Melody Ulrich's house on the other side of his neighborhood.

He didn't even ask Dad for a ride. He barely stopped at home long enough to get his bike and put on his cold-weather face mask.

As he locks up his bike, a silver SUV pulls up, exhaust puffing from its tailpipes like Terence's breath as he biked over. Eddie hops out of the front seat, says something quickly to the driver, and hurries to Terence's side.

"You biked?" she says, hollering over the wind. "Are you insane?"

"My dad wasn't around," Terence says. It's not true.

"Come on!" Eddie jogs up the walk and rings the bell.

Melody pulls the door open instantly. "You biked?" she says to Terence, her brow knitted and her mouth twisted in derision.

"Yeah, my dad —" Terence starts to say, but Melody isn't listening.

"What is *she* doing here?" she asks, glaring at Eddie.

Eddie grins. "I'm the singer."

"The singer?" Melody says with disdain. She rolls her eyes as if to say *whatever*. "Follow me." She leads her guests along the front hall to a set of steps down to a cavernous basement.

It's set up like a recording studio, with a soundproof booth at the far end behind glass. Inside are mic stands, music stands, and a gleaming black grand piano.

"Wow," Terence says.

Eddie nods, her mouth open, speechless.

"Sit there," Melody says, gesturing briefly

toward a slim and stylish couch along one wall, and she goes into the soundproof room.

Then she begins to play. The sound fills the room from speakers in the corners and woofers set into the walls near the floor.

"Chopin's Sonata no. 3 in B Minor," Terence whispers to Eddie.

She doesn't seem to care, but Melody's playing is flawless, and for the next twenty-five minutes Terence and Eddie sit silently and listen and watch her fingers dancing across the keys, her body swaying with the music, her eyes closed like she's mid-epiphany.

When she's done, Terence waits for the last chord to fade after the furious finish and jumps to his feet, applauding.

"That was amazing!" Terence says, hurrying to the booth's door as Melody comes out, actually smiling and reddening a little in the face.

"*Merci*," Melody says, miming a little curtsey.

"I have to ask, though," Terence says, though it almost hurts to go on, "why aren't you enrolled at Hart? You'd probably get a full scholarship."

Melody's smile is gone. "Hart Arts?" she says, and quickly shakes her head, dismissive. "Zero focus on core curriculum. No thank you."

"No thank you?" Terence says, following Melody out of the studio. "But you're a genius at piano. Who needs math, right?"

"I'm no fool," she says as she stops in a basement kitchenette and pulls a bottled water from the little fridge. She leans on the counter as she drinks half the bottle. "Piano is no way to make a living. I intend to go to medical school."

"Wow," Terence says, leaning in the doorway. "What a waste."

"Anyway, you've heard enough, I assume?" Melody says.

"I mean, yeah," Terence says. "You're

amazing. Do you know any Cole Porter? Duke Ellington? Lennon/McCartney?"

Melody sets down the bottle and laughs. "I learned 'Yesterday' when I was five," she says. "I can probably muddle through."

Muddle through? Terence things. "What about jazz?"

"I'm not so interested in jazz," Melody says.

"Rock?" Terence says. "Pop? Soul? R & B?"

"No," Melody says. "No, no, and no."

"You only play classical?" Terence asks as Eddie joins them in the kitchenette. "I don't understand."

"What's not to understand?" Eddie says. "I told you this was a waste of time. Melody Ulrich is a renowned snob at Franklin. Princess Melody since kindergarten."

Melody sneers at her.

"But why did you ask me to come down and listen," Terence says, "if you're not interested in joining a band anyway?"

"Well," Melody says, ushering the two of them out of the kitchenette and toward the stairs up to the first floor, "I didn't love the idea of a kid at Franklin not knowing what a piano genius I am."

"You've got to be kidding me," Terence says, letting Melody hurry them toward the door.

When she pulls it open, the wind and snow rush in and slap Terence in the face. He and Eddie step outside.

"Now I know, I guess!" Terence shouts over the furious weather.

Melody just smiles as she closes the door in their faces.

Eddie turns to him and slowly smiles, like that cat from *Alice in Wonderland*.

"Don't say it," Terence says.

"Don't say what?" Eddie says, feigning confusion.

"'I told you so,'" Terence says.

"I wouldn't dream of it."

The SUV at the curb toots its horn.

"Hey, do you want a ride?" Eddie asks. "It's pretty nasty out."

Terence glances at the SUV and then at his bike, chained to the street sign at the corner. A ride would be good; a conversation with a mom and this *thing* with Eddie actually turning into friendship would not.

"I'll be OK," Terence says. "I like winter biking." Actually he hates it.

"Suit yourself," Eddie says. "See you tomorrow. We can tell Claude he's in the band."

"No way!"

Eddie sticks out her tongue and jogs to the car, and a moment later it pulls away from the curb and vanishes into the darkening afternoon, a cloud of exhaust lingering at the curb in its place.

"Whoever heard of a big, dumb muscle-brain playing piano anyway?" Terence mutters to himself as he climbs onto his bike.

The ride home is tough, cold, and miserable, and when he gets there Dad's on the couch with a bag of sour-cream-and-onion chips and *The A-Team* streaming on TV.

Terence crosses in front of the TV and only says, "I'll be in my room."

CHAPTER THREE

Over the next few days, Terence manages to put off recruiting a pianist despite Eddie and Luke bringing up Claude at every opportunity.

"There must be someone else," Terence says, and, "Have we talked to the kids in seventh grade? Sixth?"

"Maybe we can recruit someone out of the elementary school," Eddie jokes, crossing her arms and narrowing her eyes.

"Maybe . . . ," Terence hems.

"Come over after school," Eddie says on Friday morning as they climb off the bus in front of the school. "We can practice."

"Just us?" Terence asks.

Eddie shrugs. "Sure," she says. "Unless you found someone to play keys."

Terence shakes his head.

"OK then," Eddie says, scurrying off to her first class. "You can play my guitar while I sing!"

By four o'clock, Terence sits on a folding chair in Eddie's family room, her acoustic guitar in his lap. "Now, I'm not great at guitar," he explains as he tunes. "I can't play pop standards."

"What *do* you know on guitar?" Eddie asks.

"Beatles?" Terence says, quietly strumming with his thumb. "A couple of Paul Simon songs. Um, I know one Suzanne Vega song."

"Who?"

"Never mind," Terence says, and then adds quickly, "Oh, and some Nirvana."

Eddie frowns at him and shakes her head. "Play a Beatles song."

He thinks a moment. "'With a Little Help From My Friends?'"

Eddie nods, pleased. "Play it slowly, like the Joe Cocker version."

Terence strums the opening E chords, choppy at first like the Beatles did it, and then slows into a mellow, relaxed strum.

Eddie picks up the rhythm, tapping her foot and nodding in time, and then starts singing.

She was right, Terence decides; the Cocker version is definitely more her style than the original would have been. She has a little of Cocker's growl, but her voice is rich and smoky, not nearly as erratic and wild as his was.

Halfway through, she's really belting it out, and Luke comes and leans in the family room doorway, watching them. It's a short song, and Eddie doesn't vamp the ending. She just stops when it's over and looks at Luke.

"Well?" she says.

"That was good," he says, and then looks at Terence and adds, "Not that you contribute much."

"Thanks," Terence says.

Luke shrugs and exits.

"We can do that one, right?" Eddie says, scooting forward on the couch. "That was fun."

"Yeah, I think so," Terence says. "Your singing style would be enough to make it fit in the set I have in mind."

"Cool," Eddie says. "Maybe you're not a complete dictator after all."

"What?" Terence says. *Dictator?*

"Nothing, nothing," Eddie says. "Do another one."

Terence looks at her a minute, but she just smiles back at him. He picks out a few notes, refreshing his memory, and starts playing "Bridge Over Troubled Water."

After a few more songs, Terence leans the guitar against the front of the couch. "I should probably head home," he says.

Eddie rises to walk him to the door. "We sound pretty good."

"*You* sound pretty good," Terence says.

Eddie grins and hits him on the arm. "Can we play more tomorrow?"

"My place," Terence says. "I prefer accompanying you on piano, and I have an electric keyboard in my room."

"Cool," Eddie says. "Around lunchtime?"

Terence thinks: will he be able to get his dad out of bed by then? Dressed, even? Maybe even out of the house? "Sure," he says. "Noon."

When he gets home, he sneaks into Dad's room and sets the alarm for 9:30, just to be on the safe side.

CHAPTER FOUR

It's 9:32 when Dad plods out of his bedroom
the next morning, wrapped in his robe over
baby-blue pajama pants. "Are we doing
something today?"

"Nope," Terence says, feigning innocence.
"Why do you ask?"

"My alarm went off," Dad says, dropping
into a kitchen chair and yawning like a bear on
the first of spring. "I haven't used that thing in
months."

"I don't know," Terence says, and he places a

big mug of coffee with cream in front of
his dad. "My friend — I mean, a girl from
school — is coming over today. We're starting
a new band."

Dad's eyebrows rise as he takes a big sip of
his coffee. "Great," he says and then looks at the
coffee as if seeing it for the first time. "Did you
make this?"

Terence nods.

Dad makes an impressed face, takes another
sip, and stretches. "Well," he says, lightly
slapping the table with both hands, "I'm gonna
get dressed."

"Yes," Terence whispers to himself.

Dad does get dressed, but by 11:59, he's in
front of the TV, a bag of chips in his lap. When
the doorbell rings, Terence sighs and opens
the door.

"Hi," he says, miserable.

Eddie is, as usual, grinning. "Ready for me?"

Terence checks with Dad over his shoulder,

but the old man didn't even hear the doorbell, or is so absorbed in marathoning *Star Trek: The Next Generation,* that he can't be bothered to look up.

"Sure," Terence says, closing the door. "Come on."

Terence cleaned up his room a bit in the morning, and he takes a seat at the little bench in front of his electric piano.

Eddie sits on the edge of the bed. There's really nowhere else to sit in Terence's little bedroom.

Terence runs his fingers over the keys — it's set to organ, so he switches it to piano — and adjusts the volume.

"Any requests?"

Eddie leans forward so her head is right next to his shoulder and looks at his hands on the keys. "What do you know?"

"On piano?" Terence says. "More like what do I *not* know."

"Why are we looking for a keys player again?" she asks.

Terence shakes his head. "I play bass. I love playing bass. I play bass."

"Suit yourself," she says. "Who ever heard of a bass-playing band leader?"

"Um, Jaco Pastorius?" Terence says, looking askew at her.

"Who?"

"Google him later," Terence says. He plays the opening lines of "Yesterday" by the Beatles. "How about Paul McCartney?"

"He wasn't the *leader*," Eddie argues.

"Fine," Terence says, sighing. "Gene Simmons then."

"From Kiss?" she asks. "Are you kidding?"

Terence shrugs as he finds the broken chords to open Kiss's classic "Beth."

Eddie says, "My mother loves that song."

"Mine too." Terence bites his lip at the memory.

Eddie leans back. "You have to clean the aura in here now," she says. "Play Cole Porter or Gershwin or something, quick."

Terence manages a smile and starts in on "I Won't Dance."

"Jerome Kern," Eddie says, standing up. "That works." And after a beat, she launches into the song. After a couple of lines, she elbows Terence. "Take it!" she shouts.

Terence shakes his head. The song is a duet, strictly speaking, but Frank Sinatra and so many others recorded it alone. Eddie won't let up, so Terence — quietly — takes a verse, Eddie grinning at him the whole time.

His face goes red as he finishes the phrase, but he can't help smiling as he looks down at the keys and shakes his head again.

Eddie elbows him once more as she take on the vocals, and when she finishes the song, she grabs his shoulder. "That was pretty good!"

"Nah," Terence says.

"Look, you're not Nat King Cole," she says, "but it wasn't bad."

"Gee, thanks," Terence says, crossing his arms.

Eddie shrugs, and a moment later Dad appears in the doorway, scowling a little. "Hey, turn the radio down a notch, OK? I can hardly hear the TV in there." With that, he walks away.

Eddie looks at Terence, her eyebrows up, and then bursts into laughter. Terence laughs too.

"He thought we were the radio!" Eddie says through her laughter, wiping her eyes. "That's pretty good!"

"But," Terence says, almost breathless, "I told him you were coming over to play music."

Eddie laughs even more, and Terence catches his breath.

"He wasn't even listening!" Terence says. "He's barely even here!"

That makes Eddie crack up, but just for a moment, because Terence isn't laughing anymore. He's slumped on the piano bench, shoulders drooping, hands folded on his lap.

"Hey, hey, Terry," Eddie says, putting a hand on his arm. "You OK?"

"Ever since Mom died, Dad is just . . . ," Terence starts, staring at his hands. "It's like he's just checked out."

Tears fill his eyes and, before he can bat them away, drop onto his hands like giant raindrops.

Eddie eases onto the bench beside him and puts an arm around his shoulders. "I didn't know," she says.

"I don't like to talk about it," he says, but he can't stop himself. "I miss her. So much."

Then he's bawling, sobbing, right there at the piano with this girl he barely knows sitting next to him, comforting him.

He feels like such a fool, such a baby, and he pulls himself free and stands in the middle of the room.

"Please go now," he says, surprised at how

angry his own voice sounds. "I told you I'm not looking for a friend."

"Terry—" she says, reaching for him.

"Go!" Terence snaps, and Eddie jumps up from the bench and hurries from the room. A moment later, he hears the front door slam.

Terence drops onto his bed and cries.

CHAPTER FIVE

Terence spends much of Sunday imitating Dad. He stays in bed as much as possible, watches sitcoms on the laptop in his room, and ignores a couple of text messages from Eddie.

Well, that last part isn't an imitation of Dad, obviously.

On Monday morning, Terence has been in and out of sleep for almost two solid days. He wakes up to the theme song to his favorite show, *The X-Files*, which has been marathoning on his laptop all night. That explains the dream he had about Mom and Agent Mulder skulking through a foggy forest with flashlights.

Terence sits up and closes the streaming tab in his browser and sees a new email too. It's from Eddie, and an MP3 is attached. The only text in the email is "keys player — listen!"

Terence almost clicks the link, but instead he closes the laptop and rolls out of bed. "Dad!" he calls through the house. No answer.

Terence pulls on a pair of jeans from the back of his desk chair and goes into the hall. "Dad," he says, thumping a fist on his father's bedroom door. "Can you drive me to school today?"

Because otherwise he has to take the bus, and that means seeing Eddie.

Dad's door opens, and there's the man himself, bearded and squinting one eye at him, the other closed tight against the angry daylight of the morning. "Why?"

"I missed the bus," Terence says.

Dad looks back into the bedroom at his clock on the nightstand. "No, you didn't."

"I plan to."

Dad sighs. "Get dressed. Go to school. Leave me alone." With that, he closes the door.

Ten minutes later, Terence is slogging on his bike through a sleety morning with the wind in his face.

"Hey." It's Eddie, of course. She's caught him between classes and snuck up from behind.

Terence doesn't turn around. He just moves to the side of the hallway and leans on someone's locker.

"You didn't reply to a single text this weekend," Eddie says.

"Sorry."

"You don't have to be embarrassed," she says quietly at his ear. He can feel her breath on his neck.

"I'm not."

Eddie is quiet for a second.

"I have to get to class," Terence says.

"You're next class is lunch," Eddie says. "Sit with me."

Terence shakes his head.

"I'm not going to lunch," he says, and quickly adds, "I'm going to the media center. I have a lot of homework to do."

"Liar."

Terence shrugs and steps away, weaving through the river of other students toward the library.

The problem with hiding during lunch in the media center is that there's no eating allowed in there, and even if there were, Terence doesn't have any food with him.

His stomach, though, is used to eating at 11:30, so at 11:32 it starts rumbling.

To distract himself, he pulls on headphones

and opens his email to check out that MP3 from Eddie.

It's solo piano. He knows the piece at once: "Für Elise," by Beethoven. Every piano student learns it at some point. He never studied piano with the top players at Hart, but he's pretty sure even he can muddle his way through it.

Still, he can tell this player is good.

Then again, Melody was good too, and can probably play "Für Elise" with her eyes closed with one hand while playing Chopin with the other hand.

Then suddenly it changes. Something just clicks, and the player starts weaving in and out of "Für Elise," threading through the song with jazzy fills, improvised little licks. It starts to swing a little, nothing like old Ludwig Van ever imagined.

By the time the finale comes along, it has a bebop, funky feel like the great jazz pianist Thelonious Monk, barely recognizable as "Für

Elise," but the themes are still there if you know what to listen for.

Terence pulls off the headphones and notices others in the media center staring at him. When he looks back, a girl stage-whispers, "You were tapping your foot."

The media specialist, Mr. W, appears next to his chair. "Loudly," he says.

Terence's face goes hot. "Sorry."

Mr. W shakes his head slowly and clicks his tongue before stepping away.

Terence clicks "reply" in his email from Eddie and writes, *Who is it?*

It only takes a moment for Eddie to reply, which means she's in the cafeteria just down the hall with her phone in her hands: *You have to meet him. Come to Paulie's tonight?*

Paulie's is the pizza place on Old Main Street. Everyone knows it, and Terence loves the pizza there. But he doesn't reply. He just closes his email and logs out of the computer.

"Dad?" Terence says when he arrives home from school. He's early. It's easy to be early getting home — even on your bike — if you sneak out before last bell.

After a quick search of the little rented house, and to Terence's complete surprise, Dad isn't home.

"I guess that means he at least got dressed today," Terence mutters to himself as he pulls out his phone. "Or he went out in his bathrobe."

Eddie has peppered Terence with texts most of the afternoon. Around now, she's probably climbing onto the bus for the ride home, maybe wondering if Terence will show up. The phone vibrates again in his hand as he looks at it.

Another from Eddie: *You're not on the bus.*

He types back: *I'm not?! Weird!*, and laughs.

Just be at Paulie's, smarty-pants, she texts back. *7 sharp!!*

Terence taps off the screen and tosses his phone onto the bed. He opens his laptop and pulls up the MP3 Eddie sent him earlier and plays it again. It really is good.

Maybe Dad will give him a ride to Paulie's.

CHAPTER SIX

Or maybe not.

At 6:45, it's dark and freezing cold as Terence
pushes his pedals against icy winds and slushy
sidewalks toward Old Main. Terence texted
Dad, and he waited as long as he could for him
to come home, but then he had no choice: if he
wanted to meet this pianist, he'd have to bike.

By the time Paulie's big neon sign comes
into view and he can smell the garlic-oil-brushed
crust, his eyes are running against the cold

and his nostrils are nearly sealed with frozen snot.

Terence pulls off his gloves to lock up his bike to the rack out front. When he's done, his fingers sting. He walks into Paulie's a little after seven, wiping his eyes and nose and blowing into his fists to warm his hands.

It seems like everyone in the little restaurant looks up at him in the doorway as he's unzipping his parka. Maybe it's just everyone at Eddie's table: Eddie, facing him with a forkful of lettuce halfway to her mouth, Luke, a woman who must be their mom, and a big guy with his back to the door.

Terence walks to their table. "Um," he says, wondering where he'll sit, "hi."

Eddie puts down her fork and grins as she stands. "You made it!" she says, and introduces him around the table. The big guy is Claude.

"Wait, *he's* the guy on the MP3?" Terence says, backing away a little. "Nope. No way."

"What MP3?" Claude says.

Terence squints at Eddie a second before turning his back on the table and heading for the door.

"Terry!" Eddie shouts. Her chair scrapes as she pushes it back to hurry after him.

Terence stops with his hand on the door handle.

"Just give him a chance," she says, a hand on his shoulder.

"Do you know two big gorillas knocked me down this morning?" Terence says without turning around.

"Who?"

"How should I know?" Terence says. "I don't know anyone at this dumb school besides you . . . and Melody Ulrich. I just know they were big dumb jerks."

"Like my brother," Eddie says.

Terence looks through the door's window at the darkness outside. It's started to snow.

"Terry, I —"

"Terence," he says.

After a moment, Eddie goes on, "Terence, sorry. Just sit and have pizza. Claude's a nice guy. He's just . . . big."

"And your brother?"

"I mean, he can be a jerk," Eddie admits, "but he won't. Not to you. Not to my friend."

Terence shoots her a glance over his shoulder at the word "friend."

"Sorry," she corrects. "My bandmate."

Terence turns around and almost laughs.

"Come on," Eddie says. "Have pizza. And no sulking, OK? My mom can't stand sulking."

"There aren't enough chairs."

But when he glances at the table, the waiter — a high school kid with a nametag that says "James" — is placing a chair between Eddie and her mom's seat for Terence.

"Oh."

"Come on."

So he does.

The pizza is great, as always, and by eight o'clock he's eaten his fill, had three Cokes, and even laughed a couple of times at Luke's stupid jokes.

When they all bundle up and step out into the frigid night, Terence thanks Eddie's mom for dinner. He heads for his bike.

"Wait a minute, Terence," her mom says, jogging after him, holding her knitted scarf over her mouth and nose. "You *biked* here?"

"He bikes everywhere," Eddie says. "He's a maniac."

"Well, not on my watch," her mom says. "We'll drive you home."

"Mom," Eddie says. "We walked."

Her mom looks at Terence a moment. "We live close," she says. "Walk your bike with us, and we can put it in the back of the SUV and drive you home from there."

"Really, it's no problem," Terence says.

"No way," Eddie's mom says. "You're coming with us. I insist."

Eddie's family lives very close, and after a five-minute walk with his bike and motley companions, Terence lets Eddie lean the bike beside the front stoop and lead him inside.

Eddie kicks off her boots. "I'm glad you joined us for pizza, at least."

"Me too," Terence admits. "And Claude seems OK, I guess."

"You guess?"

Terence laughs. "We should ask him to play with us."

Eddie nods. "I already have," she admits. "Tomorrow afternoon before jazz band in Mr. Bonk's room. I got his permission."

"Were you planning to tell me?" Terence protests.

Eddie giggles. "I just did. Is your bass still in Bonk's office."

Terence nods.

"OK then," she says as Mom comes in. "See you tomorrow!" With that, she scurries up a narrow staircase.

"OK, Terence," Mom says as she pokes around in the depths of her huge purse. "Let's see if we can get you home."

"Thanks," he says.

"I cannot . . . find . . . my car keys," she says, looking up and smiling at him just like Eddie does. "Give me one minute, OK?" She hurries down the hall into the kitchen.

Terence sits on the bottom of the steps, and from above he hears a slightly out-of-tune guitar being strummed.

It's Eddie, obviously, practicing in her room probably. She's not very good. The chord changes are uninspired and the strumming is not rhythmic. It sounds like her fingers are pretty weak too, unable to hold the strings tight against the fret board. But Terence knows that will get better with practice.

Then, though, she begins to sing. Terence doesn't recognize the song. It must be one of hers. The melody is beautiful. The lyrics — when he can make them out — are better than he would have thought.

He's on his feet, looking up the stairs, straining to hear better, when Eddie's mom comes back down the hall, jangling her keys.

"Ready, Terence?" she says, snapping his musical reverie.

"Oh, yes," he says. "Thanks again."

A few minutes later, Terence is strapped into the front seat of the Carson family's SUV, the heated seat warming him and a hot breeze blowing in his face from the gleaming dash.

His bike — the tires caked in slush — bangs around in the back.

"So, Terence," Ms. Carson says, "Meredith tells me you just started at Franklin?"

"That's right."

"You were at Hart Arts?" Ms. Carson asks. "Impressive."

"I guess," Terence says, but he's wishing she'd stop. Small talk like this can often lead to big talk, and big talk he'd much rather avoid.

"How many instruments do you play?" she asks as the SUV rolls slowly along Route 116. The roads are bad, and she can't even go the speed limit. Still, his house isn't far. This might be OK.

"Five, altogether," Terence says. "Some better than others."

"That is amazing," Ms. Carson says. "I'm so proud of my kids for staying interested in music. Though I don't know if Luke will stick with his sax much longer."

No great loss there, Terence thinks.

"So why did you leave Hart?" Ms. Carson says as she turns onto 18th Avenue.

Maybe he can get out here and bike the rest.

"Oh, um," Terence says, "we just couldn't

afford the tuition anymore. It's pretty — I mean, really expensive."

"Yeah, I've heard that," Ms. Carson says, forcing a smile and glancing at Terence as the corner closest to Terence's rental house comes into view.

She turns left, and Terence leans forward in his seat. "It's the little blue one," he says, pointing through the windshield. "After the brick one on the right."

Ms. Carson pulls up to the curb and switches off the engine. "I'll help you with your bike."

"Oh, I'm fine," Terence says, climbing out.

"Don't be ridiculous," Ms. Carson says as she meets Terence at the back of the SUV and pops open the tailgate. Together they lift the filthy bike from the car and set it on the sidewalk. "There you go."

"Thanks again, Ms. Carson," Terence says, "and thanks for dinner."

"My pleasure," Ms. Carson says as Terence

pushes his bike toward the house. "And Terence? If you ever need anything, you let us know, OK?"

"O-OK," Terence stammers.

"Eddie told me about your mother," Ms. Carson adds quickly, practically shouting across the yard to him. "I'm very sorry."

Terence stops and looks at the gray muck clinging to his bike tires. He never knows what to say when grown-ups apologize for his mom being dead, like it's their fault, or like they stepped on his toe.

So he doesn't say anything. He just waits a moment, and then she says, "Well, goodbye, Terence. Very nice to meet you."

"Bye," Terence manages to push out, and he watches as she climbs back into the SUV and drives slowly away.

"You know, Terence," Mr. Bonk says, his arms folded high across his chest, his chin up and his mustache shaking ferociously, "if it's a band you're looking for, we've got one here at Franklin Middle. You remember, don't you?"

"I know," Terence says, wishing Eddie and Claude would show up so he could edge his way out of this awkward conversation. "I just don't think I'll have the time, and —"

"Hey, Mr. Bonk!" Eddie bellows as she shoves through the double doors to the band room. Claude trails a few steps behind her, his mouth half open, his hair a mop over his bulging forehead.

Terence can hardly believe this is the same boy who played that amazing rendition of "Für Elise."

"Ms. Carson," Mr. Bonk says as his shoulders sag. "You have fifteen minutes."

"Thanks, Mr. B!" Eddie says as the walrusy teacher steps into his office and closes the door.

"He does *not* like me," Terence says.

"Really?" Eddie says, grinning. "'Cause I'm

pretty sure I just chased him out of the room by saying hi."

"He's not a big fan of mine, either," Claude says as he settles onto the piano bench at the front of the room. As if to punctuate his speech, he runs rapid-fire through a couple of jazzy scales. "He learned a few weeks ago that I play but never joined band."

"Why didn't you?" Terence says as he plugs in his bass.

Claude shrugs as he plays the opening to "Straight, No Chaser." "I have football practice every afternoon in the fall," he says, staring straight ahead, as if he's not just banging out a Thelonious Monk classic like it's nothing, "and hockey practice all winter."

Terence picks up the bass part, and they jam on the old jazz standard for a minute. But while the song got some lyrics in the 1980s — thirty years after Monk wrote the instrumental version — most singers don't know them.

"OK, let's bring Eddie in," Terence says over the music, and Claude stops, clinks a few keys idly, and then launches into a jaunty, up-tempo chord change. Terence picks up the strolling bass line.

Eddie looks confused.

"'All of Me!" Terence calls to her over the music, and as it dawns on her she nods, her eyes wide, and then she sings, her voice somewhere between Billie Holliday and Sarah Vaughn: raspy, but with Vaughn's power and bombast.

Eddie snaps her fingers as she paces between Terence and Claude's piano. Before long, Mr. Bonk's door opens and he stands in the doorway, shaking his head to the rhythm, a sorrowful frown on his face, forlorn that none of this trio are in his jazz band.

"All right, that was great," Terence says when the song ends.

Mr. Bonk waves dismissively at the new bandmates and retreats into his office again.

"Yeah, that was fun," Claude says. "You guys ever do anything a little . . ."

"More rock?" Terence finishes for him, and Claude nods. "Like what?"

Claude chews his cheek, staring past Terence. He really does look like a big dumb kid, but Terence is starting to see how deceiving appearances can be.

A flash of recognition crosses Claude's face, and he quietly sounds out a couple of chords before banging them out like a honky-tonk maniac.

"We need a guitar for that!" Terence says over the din.

"Fake it!" Claude shouts back, smiling a little.

And Terence does his best, which might not be enough, since Claude is playing the opening chords of Led Zeppelin's "South Bound Saurez." That means Terence has to somehow play John Paul Jones's thumping bass line at the same time as Jimmy Page's sliding and syncopated riff.

That means he has to knock the E string on every sixteenth note, while his pinky works on the higher strings to do a passable imitation of Page's guitar. It's not ideal.

To his surprise, though, just as he hits the first chord change, Eddie steps between him and Claude and belts out an amazing Robert Plant impression.

It sounds pretty good.

In fact, it sounds *great*.

They're halfway through — Terence and Claude almost laughing at Eddie's vocal a ntics — when Mr. Bonk appears again, this time far less impressed and waving his arms over his head.

Eddie stops singing. Terence stops playing. Claude keeps on, since his back is to Bonk's door. He looks at Terence, confused, as he reaches the guitar solo and starts in on a wild improvisation of his own.

"Claude Viateur!" Mr. Bonk shouts.

Claude stops and turns around on the bench. "Oh, sorry. Is our time up?"

Mr. Bonk's face is red enough to pop, Terence thinks.

"Um, yes," Terence says, dropping to one knee and unplugging his bass. "Packing up now, Mr. Bonk."

Mr. Bonk stares the three bandmates down for a moment before heading back into his office, mumbling under his breath something about "rock and roll *garbage*" as he closes the door.

"So you're in?" Terence says, walking between Eddie and Claude up the ramp toward the exit. His bass hangs from one shoulder in its gig bag, Mr. Bonk having made him take it with him this time.

Terence and Eddie will have to catch the late bus in an hour. Claude has to hurry to the gym to change for hockey practice.

"Yeah," Claude says. "It could be fun, and I

don't get any time to play what I like. My folks have me practicing sonatas all the time with Ms. Kilpatrick."

"*Arlene* Kilpatrick?" Terence says.

"You know her?" Claude asks, surprised.

"Sure, she teaches at Hart," Terence says, remembering Kilpatrick's wicked Advanced Theory course from that fall.

"She's tough," the boys say at the same time.

Terence laughs.

Eddie gives him a shove with her shoulder. "Don't forget the band rule," she says.

"What?" Terence says.

"You know," Eddie says. "The *one rule.*"

Terence thinks a minute and remembers. "Right," he says firmly. "Not looking for friends."

Claude glances at Eddie. "OK then," he says.

At the top of the ramp, he heads toward the gym. "See you guys," he says.

"Have fun!" Eddie calls after.

Friends or not, Terence is pleased. His band is starting to come together, and with players more talented than he ever imagined he'd find at a public school.

So when he bumps into another kid in the glare of sunshine through the glass front doors, he's smiling. "Oh, excuse me," he says as he looks up —

— right into the faces of his two bullies from the other morning.

"Oh," he says, backing away. "Look, guys, I —"

But they're not interested in chatting. With two hands, one of them shoves him backward, so he stumbles at the top of the ramp and falls onto his butt. His bass lands next to him with a thud. Terence hopes it's not damaged.

"Hey!" Eddie says, running to help him. But the other bully grabs her by the wrist and moves her aside.

"Just mind your own business, *Edward*," he

says as his partner in crime moves in on Terence, kicking his foot.

"You gonna get up?" the bully asks.

Terence shakes his head.

"That's what I thought," he says. "Didn't we tell you we don't want to see you around here anymore?"

"Yeah," says the one who has Eddie by the wrist. "Go back to Harts and Farts."

"Jerks!" Eddie says, trying to pull her wrist away. The bullies just laugh at her.

"Now, how are we gonna punish this weirdo for not following our orders?" says the bully standing over Terence.

As he leans down, his fists primed, Terence covers his face and closes his eyes.

"You're not," comes a deep and terrifying voice.

Terence opens his eyes, and there's Claude standing between the two bullies with one giant, piano-playing hand on each of their throats. The bullies' eyes are wide in terror, though it doesn't look like he's squeezing hard.

He must have a reputation, then.

"Understand?" Claude says.

The bullies nod and gasp "yes," and when he releases them, they bolt down the hall and out of sight.

"You OK?" he says, helping Terence up.

"I think so," Terence says. "Um, thanks."

"Sure," Claude says, clapping his hands together as if dusting them off. "That's what friends are for, right?"

Claude grins and corrects himself, "I mean bandmates."

Eddie laughs and grabs Terence's arm. "Come on," she says. "You're making Claude late for hockey practice."

Claude gives Terence a light punch on the shoulder before hurrying away again.

"So?" Eddie says.

"So?" Terence says.

"Maybe we're friends a *tiny* bit?" Eddie says, her smile and eyes twinkling.

Terence adjusts the strap of his gig bag on his shoulder. "A tiny bit," he admits, and he lets himself smile as the two of them step outside into the chilly and sunny winter afternoon to wait for the late bus.

MUSIC TRIVIA

Think you have what it takes to join Terence Kato's band? Take this music trivia quiz and find out!

1. What is the level and intensity of sound measured in?
   A. Decibels
   B. Gigabytes
   C. Vibrato

2. A musical scale comprises how many notes?
   A. 16
   B. 8
   C. 10

3. What term describes people singing without instruments?
   A. Solo
   B. Allegro
   C. A cappella

4. What term describes the section of a song that is repeated after each verse?
   A. Beat
   B. Chorus
   C. Choir

5. What term describes how high or low a musical sound is?
   A. Pitch
   B. Range
   C. Volume

6. What is the highest singing voice called?
   A. Baritone
   B. Tenor
   C. Soprano

7. How many musical instruments make up a quartet?
   A. 4
   B. 14
   C. 8

8. What Italian word means "growing louder?"
   A. Crescendo
   B. Bass
   C. Allegro

9. What are all instruments that are played by being hit with something called?
   A. Brass
   B. Woodwinds
   C. Percussion

10. What is the lowest singing voice called?
    A. Baritone
    B. Tenor
    C. Soprano

STEVE BREZENOFF

Steve Brezenoff is the author of more than fifty middle-grade chapter books, including the Field Trip Mysteries series, the Ravens Pass series of thrillers, and the Return to the Titanic series. He's also written three young-adult novels, *Guy in Real Life*; *Brooklyn, Burning*; and *The Absolute Value of -1*. In his spare time, he enjoys video games, cycling, and cooking. Steve lives in Minneapolis with his wife, Beth, and their son and daughter.